Just In Case
You Ever
Wonder

Jenna, Andrea, and Sara,
this book is for you—just in case you ever wonder.
—M. L.

To Alexa, Lizzy, and the O'Keefes with thanks.
—R. K.

Text © 1992 by Max Lucado
Illustrations © 2001 by Rosanne Kaloustian

Published in Nashville, Tennessee, by Tommy Nelson®, a division of Thomas Nelson, Inc.

Library of Congress Cataloging-in-Publication Data
Lucado, Max.
    Just in case you ever wonder / by Max Lucado ; illustrations by Rosanne Kaloustian.
        p. cm.
    Summary: A parent tells a child how special she is, both to the parent and to God.
    ISBN 0-8499-7612-X
  [1. Parent and child--Fiction. 2. Christian life--Fiction.] I. Kaloustian, Rosanne, ill. II. Title.

PZ7.L9684 Ju 2001
[E]--dc21

                                                                00-066854

Printed in China
06 07 08 PHX 9 8 7 6

MAX LUCADO

Just In Case You Ever Wonder

Illustrated by Rosanne Kaloustian

Tommy
NELSON®

Thomas Nelson, Inc.
Nashville

Long, long ago God made
a decision—

a very important decision…
one that I'm really glad He made.

He made the decision to make you.

The same hands that made the stars *made you.*

The same hands that made canyons *made you.*

The same hands that made trees and the moon and the sun *made* you.

That's why you are so special.
God made you.

He made you in a very special way.

He made your eyes so they
would twinkle.

He made your mouth so you
could smile.

He made your laugh so you
could giggle.

God made you like no one else.

If you looked all over the world—
in every city, in every house—there
would be no one else like you…

no one with your eyes,

no one with your mouth,

no one with your laugh.

You are very, very special.

And since you are so special,
God wanted to put you in just the
right home…

    where you would be warm
      when it's cold,

    where you'd be safe when
      you're afraid,

    where you'd have fun and learn
      about heaven.

So, after lots of looking for just
the right family, God sent
you to me.

And I'm so glad He did.

I'll never forget the first time I saw you...

your eyes were closed,

your fingers were curled in two
little fists,

your cheeks were puffy and round.

I knew in my heart God had sent
someone very wonderful for me to
take care of.

Your first night with me I heard every
sound you made:

I heard you gurgle,

I heard you sniff,

I heard your little lips smack.

I heard you cry when you wanted
to eat, and I fed you.

You're bigger now and do more things.

You can walk and run.

You can play and talk.

You can eat and sing and look
at books.

You're not a little baby anymore.

But as you grow and change, some things will stay the same.

I'll always love you.

I'll always hug you.

I'll always be on your side.

And I want you to know that…
just in case you ever wonder.

Remember I'm here for you.

On dark nights when you hear noises
in your closet, call me.

When you see monsters in the
shadows, call me.

On hard days when kids are mean
and don't treat you like they should,
come to me.

If you're feeling sad because your grades are bad, come to me . . . 'cause I love you.

And I always will, just in case you ever wonder.

Most of all, I'll be here to teach you about God.

He loves you.

He protects you.

He and His angels are always watching over you.

And God wants me to make
sure you know about heaven. It's a
wonderful place.

There are not tears there.

No monsters.

No mean people.

You never have to say "good-bye,"

or "good night,"

or "I'm hungry."

You never get cold or sick or afraid.

In heaven you are so close to God that He will hug you, just like I hug you.

It's going to be wonderful.

I will be there, too. I promise. We will be there together, forever.

Remember that...

just in case you ever wonder.